JoJo & BowBow

SPRING BREAK DOUBLE TAKE

BY JOJO SIWA

nickelodeon

AMULET BOOKS

PUBLISHER'S NOTE: This is a work of fiction. Names, characters, places, and incidents are either the product of the author's imagination or used fictitiously, and any resemblance to actual persons, living or dead, business establishments, events, or locales is entirely coincidental.

Cataloging-in-Publication Data has been applied for and may be obtained from the Library of Congress.

ISBN 978-1-4197-5472-2

Text copyright © 2021 JoJo Siwa
Cover and illustrations copyright © 2021 Abrams Books
© 2021 Viacom International Inc. All rights reserved. Nickelodeon and all related titles and logos are trademarks of Viacom International Inc.

Book design by Brenda E. Angelilli

JoJo Siwa is a trademark of JoJo Siwa Entertainment, LLC.

Published in 2021 by Amulet Books, an imprint of ABRAMS. All rights reserved. No portion of this book may be reproduced, stored in a retrieval system, or transmitted in any form or by any means, mechanical, electronic, photocopying, recording, or otherwise, without written permission from the publisher.

Printed and bound in the United States
10 9 8 7 6 5 4 3 2 1

Amulet Books are available at special discounts when purchased in quantity for premiums and promotions as well as fundraising or educational use. Special editions can also be created to specification. For details, contact specialsales@abramsbooks.com or the address below.

Amulet Books® is a registered trademark of Harry N. Abrams, Inc.

ABRAMS The Art of Books
195 Broadway, New York, NY 10007
abramsbooks.com

CONTENTS

NO LONGER PROPERTY OF
ANYTHINK LIBRARIES/
RANGEVIEW LIBRARY DISTRICT

CHAPTER 1

"Hi, Siwanatorz!" JoJo smiled brightly at the camera as her best friend, Miley, filmed on her phone. "As you can see, I'm somewhere unusual today." JoJo opened her arms wide, as if to say, *ta da!* "I'm on an airplane! That's because I'm on my way to London."

From behind the phone, Miley let out a squeal of excitement. "Oops, sorry," Miley whispered.

JoJo giggled. "That squeal came from none other than my best friend in the entire world. Say hi, Miley!" Miley flipped the phone and waved sheepishly into the camera. "I'm just a little excited," she admitted. "I've never been to Europe before!"

"You're going to love it," JoJo's mom assured her. "Oh wait—are you filming right now? Am I not supposed to be talking?"

"Say hi to the Siwanatorz, Mom," JoJo said with a laugh.

Her mom waved to the camera. At that moment, BowBow's tiny head popped up from her pink, sequined travel bag. She gave a disgruntled yip.

"Aw, don't worry, BowBow," JoJo cooed. "I didn't forget about you." JoJo held her adorable Yorkie up to the camera. "You're our V-I-P! Very Important Pup!"

BowBow licked JoJo's nose. Then she leapt back into her bag. JoJo couldn't blame her. BowBow's doggie bag had the softest silk bed. JoJo would cuddle up on it too, if she'd fit!

"So here's what's happening, Siwanatorz," JoJo continued. "I'm performing two spring break shows in London this week, and I'm going to take you guys behind the scenes! You'll get to see what happens *before* the curtain opens. The dress rehearsals, the hair and makeup . . ."

"The drama," Miley added with a giggle.

"Miley's right," JoJo admitted. "There's always *some* kind of last-minute drama. Like the time my best dancer, Tasha, sprained her ankle in dress rehearsal. Or the time we couldn't get the sound in the arena to work . . ."

"Oh, girls!" Mrs. Siwa chided. "There is not going to be any drama in London."

JoJo exchanged a look with Miley. "Uh-oh, Mrs. Siwa," Miley said. "I really hope you didn't just jinx us."

Mrs. Siwa shook her head. "There are no such things as jinxes."

"I guess we'll just have to see, won't we?" JoJo winked into the camera. She loved imagining all the kids that would watch this video once she posted it. "The best part of this behind-the-scenes tour is that you guys will be the first people to see my extra-special costume. It was made by my two favorite designers: Goldie Chic, and one of my best friends, Kyra Gregory. You guys are going to love it!"

Suddenly, the loudspeaker crackled. The captain's voice filled the plane. "We are now beginning our descent into London. Please disconnect your Wi-Fi, and make sure your seat backs and tray tables are in their full upright position."

JoJo gave her Siwanatorz a final wave. "See you all in London!" She quickly posted the video online, before disconnecting the Wi-Fi on her phone. At home, she liked to edit her videos and add things like music and sound effects. But she wanted her behind-the-scenes tour to be completely natural and in real time.

"I can't believe I'm about to be in England!" Miley said, her voice filled with awe.

JoJo squeezed her friend's hand. "I'm proud of you, Miley. The last time we flew in a plane, you were so nervous. But look at you now!"

Miley grinned at her. "I guess it gets easier each time. Plus, I'm too excited to be nervous. I can't wait to see Big Ben! And the

River Thames! And shop on Oxford Street! And hear all the British accents! I've read my guidebook so many times I practically memorized it."

Outside, the plane cut through the clouds. A faint city skyline appeared below. JoJo leaned over Miley. Both girls pressed their foreheads to the window. "You ready for this?" JoJo asked her friend.

"London, here we come," Miley said.

Two hours later, JoJo, Miley, and Mrs. Siwa were dragging their suitcases into The Worchester Hotel. From the outside, the hotel looked like it was straight out of a history book: an old, red, stately building, with flags fluttering above the entryway. But inside, everything was sparkly and new. Huge chandeliers shimmered from the ceilings. Elaborately carved gold tables held vases overflowing with flowers. Everywhere you looked, the hotel staff bustled past in matching navy blue suits. Someone whisked their bags away, and someone else offered them sparkling water off a silver tray.

"Thank you," JoJo said, as she took one of the crystal glasses off the tray. Several slices of lemon and strawberries floated in the water.

"Even the water is fancy here," Miley said.

JoJo took a sip. "And delicious!"

"I'm going to go check in," Mrs. Siwa told the girls. "Do you think you two can make yourself comfortable for a few minutes?"

JoJo eyed the hotel lobby's velvet couches, filled with fluffy pillows. Music played quietly in the background, and a soft breeze blew in from an open terrace. "Yeah, I think we can make do," she joked.

"This place is *ah*-mazing," Miley exclaimed as they settled into one of the couches.

BowBow stuck her head out of her bag and yipped in agreement.

"What a precious dog," said a man with a British accent. He had silver hair and was wearing the navy blue suit that all hotel staff wore. He carried the same type of silver tray that their water had been on, but his tray was filled with dog treats. "Welcome to The Worchester Hotel," he said. "I'm Samuel, one of the porters here. We carry bags and help guests. But I get to do the best job of all. I get to welcome our most important guests: our canine ones!"

BowBow hopped onto JoJo's lap and let out an excited yip at the sight of the dog treats. "See, BowBow," JoJo said. "I told you that you were a V-I-P!"

"She's a V-I-P?" Samuel repeated.

"Yes," JoJo explained. "A Very Important Pup!"

"Ah! So she is. For our V-I-P, I can offer a B-O-N-E." Samuel held the silver tray out to BowBow with a flourish.

As BowBow gobbled up her treat, Miley suddenly elbowed JoJo. "Do you see who I see?" she asked.

JoJo followed her friend's gaze to the elevator bank. Stepping off the elevator was a very familiar face. "No way!" JoJo gasped. "Is that *Tad Harwell?*" She tried not to stare, because she of all people knew what it was like to be stared at. But she couldn't help it! Tad Harwell was the star of the *Nine Lives* movie trilogy. He was only a few years older than them, but already one of the most famous actors in Hollywood. JoJo knew all about him because one of her best friends, Grace, was a *Nine Lives* superfan. She'd read each book eight times, and could quote every line from the first two movies.

"Grace is going to freak out when we tell her," Miley whispered.

"Seriously," JoJo replied.

Samuel glanced over at Tad. "Oh yes," he whispered conspiringly. "Many actors and musicians visit The Worchester." He winked at JoJo as he said it. She smiled back. Samuel clearly recognized her, but was too polite to say anything.

"Um, JoJo," Miley said suddenly. "Am I seeing things . . . or is Tad walking straight toward us?"

"You are not seeing things," JoJo whispered back.

"Hey, there," Tad said as he stopped in front of them. He laughed, and JoJo realized they must look as starstruck as she felt.

"Hi," she said, her voice squeaking a little.

"You're Tad Harwell!" Miley blurted out. Her face reddened, and she cleared her throat.

"I am." Tad smiled the dimpled smile he was famous for. His bright blue eyes sparkled. "And you are JoJo Siwa."

JoJo nodded mutely. *Tad Harwell* knew who she was? For the first time in her life, she couldn't seem to muster up a single word!

"My little sister, Poppy, is a huge fan," Tad continued. "She's out running an errand with our mom right now, but she's going to lose it when she finds out I met you, JoJo. Poppy was actually just telling me that you're performing in London this week, and have an extra-special costume."

"Wow," JoJo finally managed to say. "She must have watched my last video. Sounds like she's a real Siwanator!"

"She's pretty mad that we can't make it to either of your shows while we're here," Tad said. "But my schedule is so jam-packed with filming."

"What are you filming?" Miley asked eagerly.

"I'm in town filming the final installment of the *Nine Lives* trilogy. Do you guys know it?"

"*Know it?*" Miley squealed. "Our friend Grace has made us watch the first two movies a million times!"

"Tad, this is my friend, Miley," JoJo said quickly. She shot Miley an apologetic look. She'd been so starstruck, she forgot to introduce her best friend! Luckily, Miley seemed to understand.

"Nice to meet you, Miley." Tad flashed her his dimpled smile. "JoJo, I hate to do this but . . . would you mind taking a photo with me for my sister?"

"Yeah, sure," JoJo said. She tried to play it cool, but inside she was shrieking with excitement.

"I can help with that," Samuel offered. He'd been standing so quietly to the side that JoJo had almost forgotten he was there! But now he took Tad's phone from him. JoJo scooped BowBow up in her arms. She knew her fans loved when BowBow was in a picture with her.

"Smile!" The camera on Tad's phone clicked.

"Perfect," Tad said, admiring the photo. "My sister will love it. Now how about if we all take a photo together?" He gestured for Miley to join.

Miley jumped off the couch faster than JoJo had ever seen her move. JoJo had to bite her tongue to keep from laughing.

"Do you mind, Samuel?" JoJo asked, handing him her phone.

"Not at all," Samuel said. "Everyone say . . . London!"

13

"London!" JoJo, Miley, and Tad cheered as the camera clicked.

Tad glanced at his watch. "I better go. My call time is soon. But thanks again, JoJo and Miley. It was very nice to meet you both."

"Bye!" JoJo and Miley called after him. As soon as he was out of sight, Miley grabbed JoJo's hands and jumped up and down.

"Can you believe—?" Miley said at the same time as JoJo said, "I can't believe—!"

Both girls burst out laughing. "One thing's for sure," JoJo said. "This trip is off to an amazing start!"

CHAPTER 2

*B*eep! Beep!

JoJo groaned as her alarm clock cut into the amazing dream she'd been having. In her dream, BowBow had learned to sing, and they were performing together for the entire *Nine Lives* cast at Royal Albert Hall—the very venue JoJo was scheduled to perform at that night. JoJo opened one eye and squinted into the sunlight that streamed in through a crack in the hotel room's curtains. She, Miley, and BowBow had been so jet-lagged after their flight that they'd decided to take quick catnaps. Or, a quick doggie nap in BowBow's case. Now, as BowBow jumped into her bed to cuddle with her, JoJo wished it didn't have to be quite so quick.

Miley rolled over in the king-size bed they were sharing. "Our nap is over already?" she mumbled into her pillow. "Why do I feel like it's the middle of the night?"

"Welcome to being jet-lagged," JoJo said. She did a quick calculation. It was 1 P.M. here, but London was eight hours ahead of Los Angeles. "It's five A.M. back home."

Miley sat up and stretched. "My body is so confused."

"Tell me about it," JoJo said with a yawn.

JoJo's mom threw open the door that connected their two hotel rooms. "Rise and shine, sleepy heads!" she said cheerfully. "We have to get to the venue." Mrs. Siwa smiled brightly as she pulled opened a blue velvet curtain. Sunlight poured into the hotel room through the terrace doors.

"I'm blinded!" JoJo squealed, shielding her eyes. But as she slowly adjusted to the light, she couldn't resist going over to admire the terrace. It looked out over The Worchester's incredible garden, complete with rose trellises, manicured hedges, and a whole fruit and vegetable section. In the distance was a view of a neighborhood filled with brightly colored brownstones. "It looks like a rainbow of buildings," JoJo said. "That's my kind of place!"

Miley hopped out of bed and came to join her. "That's Notting Hill," she said. "According to my guidebook, it's one of the most popular tourist destinations in London."

"There was even a rom-com made about it with Julia Roberts," Mrs. Siwa chimed in.

"And it's right outside our window," JoJo said. "Not too shabby!"

"The inside of our hotel room isn't so shabby either," Miley said. She flipped a light switch and a crystal chandelier turned on. "Can you believe our hotel room has its own chandelier? And its own sitting area, and a bathroom that's bigger than my bedroom back home!"

"I never want to leave!" JoJo said. She went over to the sitting area. Two blue velvet couches flanked a beautiful glass and gold table. A huge basket of fruit and chocolate sat on the table. It was a gift to JoJo from the hotel.

JoJo grabbed a mini hazelnut-chocolate bar from the basket and tossed another one to Miley. "I could get used to waking up to this kind of treatment," Miley said with a giggle.

"Enjoy your chocolate, girls. Then it's time to get a move on," Mrs. Siwa said. "JoJo's show starts at seven P.M., and we still have to get to the venue, and then do sound check, and dress rehearsal, and JoJo needs her hair and makeup done—"

"Don't worry, Mom," JoJo cut in. "This isn't my first rodeo—or concert," she added with a grin. "I promise we'll get everything done in time."

"You are the pro." Her mom grinned back at her. "I'll meet you in the hallway in ten minutes," she added, before disappearing into her room.

While Miley got ready in the bathroom, JoJo went over to her special garment bag. Her parents had given it to her for her birthday last year. It was bright pink with gold trim, and had her name embroidered on the front in big, rainbow-colored letters. Carefully, she unzipped the bag. Her super-secret costume was tucked inside, in all of its glittery glory. JoJo ran a finger over its colorful sequins and feathers. She shivered with excitement as she imagined wearing it onstage later that night. She allowed herself one last moment to admire it before zipping the bag back up.

"Are you ready to go, BowBow?" JoJo asked, scooping her dog up in her arms. BowBow licked her nose. Then, with a yip, she leapt out of JoJo's arms and raced to the door. JoJo laughed. "I'll take that as a yes. You have the most exciting day out of all of us. You get to be primped and pampered at The Worchester's world-famous doggie spa."

"According to my guidebook, people travel to The Worchester from all over just to take their dogs to this spa," Miley said.

"You're going to love it, BowBow!" JoJo said.

Her dog barked and wagged her tail. The instant JoJo opened their hotel room door, BowBow sprinted into the hallway.

"It looks like someone is excited for her spa day," Mrs. Siwa said as she joined them. They all followed BowBow to the elevator bank. Nearby, a sign showed a picture of a small red bus with The Worchester's name emblazoned on the side. *Enjoy a guided tour of London, just for guests of The Worchester,* JoJo read. *Hotel tour buses depart at 9 a.m. daily.*

"I can't wait until *we* get to tour London tomorrow!" JoJo said. She had a full day and night off between her two shows—and she and Miley already had a long list of sights they wanted to see.

The elevator door opened, and BowBow pranced inside. "Which floor do we want, girls?" Mrs. Siwa asked.

JoJo pushed a button that said PP. "That stands for Pampered Pooch," she explained. "It's the name of the doggie spa!"

The elevator rose up and up. Finally it opened onto the penthouse floor. "Whoa," Miley said.

Behind glass doors was a beautiful room filled with dozens of white silk dog beds. Poodles and Pomeranians and bichons galore lounged on the beds, while manicurists painted the dogs' nails. Off to the side was a row of porcelain bathtubs filled with bubble baths, and a massage table where an enormous golden retriever was receiving a doggie massage. There was even an indoor playground, complete with a doggie slide and doggie hammocks. "Those really are some pampered pooches!" Mrs. Siwa said. BowBow dashed out of the elevator and started barking with delight.

"Hello!" a woman called out from behind a sleek, metal counter. "I'm Michelle, and I can help check in your Pampered Pooch. Who do we have here?"

"This is BowBow," JoJo said. "She's very happy to be here, if you can't tell."

"Well, we are just as happy to have her!" Michelle said. She consulted her computer. "It looks like we have BowBow signed up for the full works: a perfumed bubble bath, followed by a manicure and massage. She'll finish with our rejuvenating doggie facial. It's guaranteed to make your dog feel as young as a puppy again!"

BowBow lifted onto her hind legs and barked wildly. "It sounds like she's ready to get started," Michelle said with a laugh. "Just one very important question first. Would BowBow prefer a glitter pink nail polish or a matte purple nail polish?"

"Which do you like better, BowBow?" JoJo asked her dog, pointing at the nail polish colors displayed on the counter.

BowBow let out two sharp barks.

"I agree," JoJo said. "Glitter pink it is!" She kissed her pup on the head. "Have the best day ever, BowBow! We'll pick you up before the show!" she called out as a woman in a pink uniform whisked her dog away.

"I have a feeling she will," Mrs. Siwa said. "Now we better get going with our day, girls. We have a show to put on!"

CHAPTER 3

"**S**ay something, JoJo," the sound technician instructed. JoJo was standing on the stage, doing the final sound check for her show. In less than two hours, she'd be performing live right here in London's iconic Royal Albert Hall.

"Hello, London!" JoJo yelled into her microphone. Her voice boomed through the enormous venue. Right now, all 5,200 seats were empty. But come showtime, it would be a packed house.

"That sounded good. We're all set," the sound technician confirmed. JoJo yawned as she thanked him. She was still feeling a little jet-lagged. It was so strange to think that it was morning back home!

"Isn't it weird that it's nighttime here, but at home our families are just finishing breakfast?" Miley asked as she joined her onstage.

"I was just thinking the same thing!" JoJo exclaimed. "It's like you read my mind."

"Best friend telepathy," Miley replied. They sat down on the stage and let their feet dangle off the edge.

"Wow," JoJo said, looking around the huge venue. The building was a circular dome, and everything about it was fancy—from the arched windows on the top level to the float-ing, white lights in the center. "This place is so cool."

"Seriously," Miley said. "According to my guidebook, Queen Victoria had it built in 1871."

"Clearly, the Queen had good taste!" JoJo pointed to the venue's beautiful glass dome roof. "It's crazy to think how many amazing singers have stood on this stage before me."

"Does it make you nervous?" Miley asked.

"Me? Nervous? Never!" JoJo tugged at her side ponytail, which was meticulously styled with a gold and pink oversize bow, thanks to Sarah, her hair and makeup artist.

"Really?" Miley squinted her eyes doubt-fully at JoJo. That was the thing about best friends: They really could read your mind, whether you liked it or not!

"Okay, okay. Maybe I'm a *tiny* bit nervous," JoJo admitted. "But performing in venues like this has always been my dream."

Miley squeezed her hand. "You've got this, girl."

"JoJo? Oh, there you two are." JoJo's mom poked her head onto the stage. "I have to meet with the venue manager for a few minutes. Do you guys need anything?"

JoJo flashed her mom a thumbs-up. "Everything's under control," she assured her. "We had our final dress rehearsal and sound check, and my hair and makeup are done. I even livestreamed most of it for my Siwa-natorz!" JoJo hopped back up to her feet and rubbed her hands together in excitement. "Now I just have to put on my super-special, super-secret costume!"

"Have you seen this costume?" Miley asked Mrs. Siwa. "Because JoJo hasn't let me take

28

a look! She wouldn't even wear it to dress rehearsal."

Mrs. Siwa shook her head. "I've only seen sketches. My daughter has guarded that costume like it's the crown jewels. I wasn't even allowed to come to the fittings!"

"That's because I want everyone to be surprised," JoJo said. "Even you two," she added, pointing at her mom and her best friend. Her mom blew her a kiss before heading off to her meeting. "I just have one stop to make before I get dressed," JoJo told Miley. She led her friend backstage, to where the dancers were busy stretching. "Hi, guys!" JoJo called out to them. The crew and dancers had all flown out on an earlier flight than JoJo. "You all know my friend Miley, right?" The dancers all waved at Miley. Miley was a great choreographer and had even choreographed some of JoJo's dances in the past. So most of the dancers had met her.

"Hey, everyone!" Miley said. "I'm excited to see your moves tonight."

"Hey, Miley!" JoJo's friend, Tasha, called out. JoJo and Tasha had met at dance class when they were just five years old. Tasha had danced in every single one of JoJo's shows so far. "Are you here to give us a pep talk, JoJo?" Tasha asked with a grin.

"You know it," JoJo replied. Her dancers liked to joke about her famous pre-show pep talks, but JoJo knew it helped get them excited to perform. It helped get her excited, too! "Guys, we are in *London*!" JoJo said. "At one of the most iconic venues in the world. I don't know about you, but this has always been a dream of mine."

"Me too!" Tasha jumped in. The other dancers echoed her.

"So you know what we're going to do?" JoJo asked. Her voice grew louder with each word. "We are going to go out on the stage, and we are going to perform like we have never performed before! We're going to knock the socks off Royal Albert Hall! Right?"

"Right!" the dancers cheered.

"GO GET IT, team!" JoJo finished. The dancers exploded with hoots and hollers. They were still clapping and cheering as JoJo headed to her dressing room to get ready.

"The moment of truth is here," Miley said. "I finally get to see your costume!"

"You, and all my Siwanatorz," JoJo said. She handed Miley her phone. "Do you mind filming this, Miley?"

"Sure," Miley said. "I'll set it up to livestream again, so your Siwanatorz can watch the reveal in real time."

31

JoJo walked over to the garment bag she'd hung in the back of her dressing room. "Lights, camera . . . action!" Miley said with a giggle.

"I'm back, Siwanatorz," JoJo announced. "And this time I'm taking you behind the scenes in my dressing room as I get ready for my show tonight. This garment bag holds the costume I've been telling you all about. This costume is really special to me, because I was so involved with the design process. I worked with two of my favorite designers— Goldie Chic and my friend, Kyra—and we created the costume of my dreams. And now I finally get to show it to you all!"

With a flourish, she unzipped the bag. "Ta da!" she said. "Isn't it a—SWEATSHIRT? Wait, what?" JoJo's heart pounded as she stared at the garment bag. Her stunning, one-of-a-kind costume was gone, and in its place was a sweatshirt. The sweatshirt was the same neon pink as her garment bag, and covered in shiny gemstones. The style was very her—except that it wasn't hers! "I don't understand." JoJo yanked the sweatshirt out. Without it, the garment bag was empty. "My costume was in this bag earlier this afternoon! I double- and triple-checked!"

"And we know that is definitely your garment bag," Miley piped up. She pointed to the big, rainbow-colored *JOJO* embroidered on the front.

"So where's my costume?" JoJo gasped. In an hour, she was supposed to be onstage in front of thousands of fans, wearing the extra-special costume she'd promised them. A costume that was now officially missing. Suddenly, JoJo realized that Miley was still filming. She cleared her throat as she turned to the camera. "Siwanatorz," she said slowly,

"It looks like we have a mystery on our hands. I guess there's going to be some drama here after all."

She waited for Miley to stop filming before mulling her options. "Looks like we're going to have to get creative," she told her friend. "The rest of my clothes are at the hotel—I don't have time to go get them before the show starts. But if there's one thing I love, it's a challenge. I'm going to bounce back; I just need to figure out *how*."

"Let me think." Miley paced through JoJo's dressing room. "We need to create a new costume from scratch, and quickly." Suddenly she stopped short. "I don't know how to do that, but I do know someone who will." She grabbed JoJo's phone. "I think we'd better make a phone call."

CHAPTER 4

"**D**on't worry, Miley—she'll pick up," JoJo whispered. She and Miley were huddled in front of JoJo's phone, their eyes glued to the FaceTime screen. As the phone rang, Bow-Bow, who was looking extra glam after a day at the spa, hopped onto JoJo's lap. JoJo kissed her dog's head. BowBow always knew just how to make her smile.

"JoJo? Are you calling me from London?"

JoJo blew out a sigh of relief as her friend's familiar face filled the screen.

"Kyra!" she exclaimed. "It's so good to see your face."

Kyra glanced at her watch. "What's going on? Aren't you supposed to be going onstage soon, JoJo?"

"That's exactly what I was going to ask."

JoJo turned around to find her mom standing in the doorway, looking very confused.

"Let's just say we've got a fashion emergency on our hands," JoJo said with a wry smile. She quickly filled Kyra and her mom in on everything that happened.

"So, the costume Goldie Chic and I designed with you is gone?"

"It's gone," JoJo told her. "Sorry, Kyra. I know you put a lot of work into that look! Now Miley and I are putting our heads together to figure out what I can wear onstage. With your eye for fashion, we figured you could help."

"Of course I'll help," Kyra reassured her. "That's what friends are for. Now, here's what you're going to do. You need to borrow anything you can find from your crew and dancers. Look for clothing and accessories that are fun and bright and very *JoJo*. Call me back when you have everything. As they say in the fashion world, we'll have to make it work!"

"Got it," Miley said.

"Sounds good to me!" JoJo exchanged confident smiles with Miley and Kyra. There was nothing she couldn't do with the help of her friends. She looked over at her mom.

"This sounds like our best option," her mom agreed.

"Thanks, Kyra," JoJo said.

"We'll fix this, JoJo," Kyra promised her. "Oh, and get glue too!" Kyra yelled, right before JoJo ended the call.

"Let's divide and conquer," JoJo's mom suggested. "I'll talk to the crew and you two talk to the dancers?"

"Good idea," Miley said. She grabbed JoJo's hand and pulled her over to where the dancers were warming up. BowBow pranced behind then.

Tasha was the first one to notice them. "What's going on?" she asked. "Why aren't you in your costume, JoJo?"

"Because my costume is missing," JoJo told her. Suddenly something occurred to her. "Actually, have any of you seen it?" She looked out at a sea of blank faces.

"Did any of you see someone carrying a costume around?" Miley added. "Or carrying a bag big enough to hold one?"

The dancers all shook their heads. "What's going on, JoJo?" Tasha asked. "Is this some kind of late April Fools' joke? Because it would be a good one!"

"It's no joke," JoJo said calmly. "My costume is definitely missing. But don't worry, we've got this."

"We need clothes and accessories that are totally JoJo's style," Miley filled in. "You know what I mean—bright, shiny . . ."

"Extra?" Tasha offered.

"Exactly." JoJo said with a grin.

"And we need them fast," Miley said.

The dancers jumped into action. They yelled over each other as they dug through their bags. "I've got an extra leotard—don't you have those leg warmers—what about Cassie's skirt—?"

Five minutes later, JoJo had a glittery pile of tulle and spandex and sequins at her feet. "Here, take this too." Cassie, her young- est dancer, dropped a gorgeous rainbow- sequined bow on the pile.

"Ooh, love that," JoJo said.

Cassie tossed her blond, side ponytail. She was two years younger than JoJo, and JoJo knew she really looked up to her. Cassie was always copying JoJo's hair and fashion. The dancers even teased her by calling her MiniJo. JoJo didn't mind, though. It was like having a little sister! Plus, Cassie was an amazing dancer. "I knew I could count on you, Cass."

Cassie beamed as JoJo and Miley scooped up the donated clothes and accessories. Bow- Bow lifted Cassie's rainbow bow in her teeth.

"Is the show going to be okay?" Cassie asked with a hint of worry.

"Thanks to you guys . . . definitely!" JoJo took a deep breath and squared her shoulders.

40

Her dancers counted on her to lead them. She couldn't let them down—costume or no costume. "Nothing has changed except that now I have another ultra special costume made with the help of my friends! We're going to go out there and rock London!"

"Yeah we are!" Tasha cheered.

"Yeah we are!" Cassie repeated.

"I'm proud of you," Miley whispered to JoJo as they hurried back to her dressing room. "You stayed strong for your dancers."

"Thanks." JoJo smiled at her best friend. "I am so glad you're here, Miley!"

"And I'm so glad Kyra is here," Miley said with a laugh, as she FaceTimed their friend. "Well, kind of here."

Kyra's face popped up on the phone's screen. "What do you have for me?" she asked.

JoJo and Miley quickly spread out

41

everything for Kyra to see. BowBow dropped Cassie's bow in front of the phone. "Rainbow sequins with a touch of dog drool," Kyra said. "Now that's fashion-forward!"

"Don't forget about me," JoJo's mom said as she joined them. She added a roll of neon-pink duct tape, a strand of battery-operated twinkle lights, and a bottle of superglue to the pile.

"Oh, and this!" Miley exclaimed. She held up the pink mystery sweatshirt for Kyra to see.

"Okay, give me a minute." Kyra carefully studied the items spread out on the floor. Then she grabbed her sketchbook and began sketching. JoJo eyed the clock as she paced nervously, BowBow prancing along behind her. She trusted Kyra's design skills more than anyone's, but the show was getting closer and closer. She exchanged a look with Miley, who seemed just as concerned. Could they really get this done in time?

"Ready!" Kyra exclaimed. She held her sketch up to the screen and quickly talked them through the design. "Mrs. Siwa, you can work on the skirt. Miley and JoJo: You guys work on the leg warmers. Everyone ready?"

"Ready," JoJo, Miley, and Mrs. Siwa said in unison.

"Yip!" BowBow barked.

"You're my hero, Kyra!" JoJo blew her friend a kiss before ending the call.

It was so silent as they worked that JoJo could hear the clock ticking away the seconds to her show. Miley frantically tore gemstones off the mystery sweatshirt, and JoJo glued them on to the leg warmers, following Kyra's design.

"Done!" JoJo said at last.

"Me too," her mom said. It was seven minutes to show time. JoJo changed and did a quick spin to show off their handiwork. Like the dancers, she wore a bright pink leotard

43

under a rainbow tulle skirt. But thanks to Kyra, her outfit didn't stop there. The battery-operated twinkle lights were knotted around her waist like a glimmering belt. The pink duct tape had been used to make a lightning bolt on her skirt, and several sparkly bows, including Cassie's rainbow-sequined one, had been glued on top of it. But the pièce de résistance was her leg warmers. They had a special message spelled out in gemstones on them: SIWA on the left leg, and NATOR! on the right. BowBow barked in excitement.

"BowBow's right," JoJo's mom said. "You look incredible, honey!"

"And those leg warmers just gave me an amazing idea for a dance move," Miley exclaimed. "I call it the Siwanator Kick." She demonstrated the move by doing a pirouette that ended by jumping in the air and kicking one leg out, then the other.

"Ooh, let me try!" JoJo said. Every part of her costume glimmered and shined as JoJo spun in a pirouette. As she jumped into the kicks, the word SIWANATOR! flashed on her legs.

"Now that's what I call a showstopper," her mom said.

JoJo glanced at the clock. "And just in the nick of time. I've got to get onstage!"

When the curtain opened on the Royal Albert Hall, revealing a packed house, JoJo was perfectly in place, surrounded by her dancers. "Hello, London!" she cheered. "I'm so, so excited to be here!"

The audience responded with their own cheers of excitement. JoJo grinned as she looked out at the crowd. She loved seeing all the kids laughing and clapping. She could feel their energy. One girl in the front row was clutching her mom's arm and squealing at the top of her lungs. JoJo couldn't help but smile. That girl did not seem the least bit bothered that JoJo wasn't wearing her super-special costume.

"I have a secret to tell you guys," JoJo said. "Something big." She lowered her voice to a whisper into the microphone, and instantly the crowd quieted. "As some of you know from watching my videos online, I was *supposed* to be wearing a super-special, top-secret costume tonight. I know you guys were probably really excited to see it. I was excited to wear it! But when I went into my dressing room earlier, my costume was missing! I have to admit: I kind of freaked at first. I had *nothing* else to wear onstage! Luckily, one of my best friends, Kyra, is an amazing fashion designer, and she helped me come up with this new costume last minute. And my other best friend, Miley, and my mom—and of course all of my dancers—helped me pull it off. And I think it turned out really cool!" JoJo did a spin. Under the lights of the stage, her costume shimmered even more brightly. "What do you guys think?"

The audience erupted with cheers. "What would we do without our BFFs, right?" JoJo said. The audience cheered even louder. She watched as several kids gave each other hugs. "Now that I have this awesome new costume, I guess I better sing in it, right?" No sooner were the words out of her mouth than the first few notes of "Boomerang" filled Royal Albert Hall. "I don't really care about what they say," JoJo sang. She broke into Miley's new dance move, ending with the Siwanator Kick. The audience went wild. "Imma come back like a boomerang . . ."

CHAPTER 5

JoJo yawned as she rolled over in bed. Beams of sunlight filtered into her hotel room. What time was it? She rubbed her eyes and looked at the clock. *Ten* A.M.*?* She glanced over at Miley, who was still fast asleep in the bed next to hers. On the floor, BowBow snored away in her sequined travel bag. JoJo couldn't believe they'd slept in! She loved to sleep late, but not when they had London to see! And they had been up late the night before.

JoJo had done an encore at her show . . . and then another one, because who could say no to a standing ovation?

JoJo sat up and stretched her arms over her head. She was glad she got to sleep in, but now she was ready to get the day started. She didn't have a show tonight, which meant she and her BFF had the whole day to play tourist.

"Wake up, Miley," JoJo said.

Miley responded with a snore.

"You asked for it." JoJo grabbed a pillow and threw it at her.

"Hey!" Miley groaned. She pulled her blanket over her head.

"Rise and shine!" JoJo said cheerfully. "It's ten A.M. and we're in London with a full day off!"

"London!" Miley popped straight up. "Ten A.M.! Day off!" She leapt out of bed and grabbed her towel. "What are you doing still in bed, JoJo?"

"Me?" JoJo exclaimed, but Miley was already in the shower.

"Hurry!" she heard Miley yell. "London is waiting for us!"

JoJo showered and got ready in record time. Fifteen minutes later, she and Miley had dropped BowBow back off at The Worchester's Pampered Pooch Doggie Spa and were sitting down to eat at the hotel's dining room. The room had the largest chandelier JoJo had ever seen and wall-to-wall windows with amazing views of London. Waiters in suits whisked past, silently filling glasses and removing empty plates.

"I asked my mom if she wanted to come to breakfast with us, but she told me I was about two hours too late for that," JoJo said with a laugh. "But she'll meet us for some sightseeing after we eat."

"I'm hungry enough to eat three breakfasts!" Miley said. She flipped open the menu. "Holy deliciousness! I'm literally drooling, JoJo. According to my guidebook, The Worchester has one of the best breakfasts in London, and I believe it!"

JoJo studied the menu choices. "Do I want strawberry Belgian french toast with a whipped cherry and fudge topping? Or chai-cinnamon scones with white chocolate shavings?"

"Or what about ricotta and chocolate-stuffed french toast, with a powdered sugar-nutmeg finish?" Miley added.

"Yum," JoJo breathed. "How are we ever going to choose?"

"Hmmm," Miley said thoughtfully. "Maybe we don't have to!"

A waiter stopped at their table. "Welcome to The Worchester, ladies," he said in a proper English accent. "I'm Benjamin, and I do hope you enjoy this complimentary strawberry-rhubarb tea, made with ingredients from The Worchester's own garden." He placed a tea kettle on the table, along with two porcelain teacups painted with beautiful pink roses.

"Those teacups are so pretty!" JoJo exclaimed.

"Yes, they're true antiques," Benjamin replied. "We have more than seventy-five patterns, one of the biggest collections in the UK."

JoJo took a sip of her tea. "Delish!" she declared.

"Double delish," Miley agreed.

"Just wait until you try the food," Benjamin said with a wink.

JoJo and Miley ordered the waffles, scones, *and* french toast. "We'll be sharing them all," JoJo said with a grin.

"A wise choice, if I do say so myself," Benjamin replied.

JoJo took another sip of tea as they waited for their food. She stuck out her pinkie and in an exaggerated British accent, said, "Cheerio, darling."

"I quite fancy this tea," Miley replied in her own British accent.

"Oh yes, it's jolly good," JoJo replied. "Brilliant, really."

Both girls were lost in a fit of giggles by the time Benjamin brought their food over.

"Triple delish," Miley said when she saw their overflowing plates.

"I need this in my belly, stat!" JoJo added.

"Jolly good," Benjamin said with a smile. "Do signal if you need anything." With a wave, he added, "Toodle-oo!"

JoJo and Miley could barely wait until he was gone to burst out laughing. "Toodle-oo!" JoJo repeated.

"Pip-pip!" Miley replied.

"Ta-ta!" JoJo added.

They were still laughing as they dug into their food. It tasted as good as it looked. "I'm finishing every last bite!" JoJo declared.

"I've never had a scone before," Miley said, "but now I want to eat one every day!"

JoJo snapped a photo of the scone to show their friend, Jacob, who was an amazing baker. "I think we found Jacob's next baking project," she said. They were quiet for a few minutes as they enjoyed their food. But as delicious as everything was, JoJo couldn't stop thinking about her costume. "I still don't understand what happened to it," she said thoughtfully as they ate. "It didn't just disappear into thin air!"

"Maybe a superfan borrowed it," Miley suggested. "Someone who really, really likes your costumes."

"No way!" JoJo exclaimed. "No one in my tour family would ever take the dress without asking, even just to borrow it. Right?"

"Not unless there's a super*foe* among us," Miley said with a giggle. "Just kidding. You're totally right, JoJo. There must be another explanation."

"How could someone even get into my dressing room?" JoJo continued. "We have a ton of security at all my shows. You need a special pass to get backstage. Only my dancers and crew are allowed. And I could never imagine anyone on my team doing something like this. They all knew how excited I was about that costume."

They were almost done with their food when Miley suddenly let out a squeal. "I spot Tad Harwell, and he's coming over to us!"

"Hey, guys," Tad said. "Was your breakfast as insanely amazing as mine?"

"More," JoJo said. "Though, I'm so full, I may never be able to dance again."

"Hey." Miley tossed a scone at JoJo. "Don't even joke about that!"

Tad laughed. "I'm heading out to film, but I just wanted to stop to say hi. Poppy isn't going to believe she missed you *again*!"

"Where are you filming today?" Miley asked.

"Buckingham Palace," Tad told them.

"That's so cool!" Miley said.

"We've filmed all over London," Tad said. "At Big Ben, the National Gallery, Royal Albert Hall—"

"That's where my show was last night," JoJo said.

"Oh believe me, I know," Tad replied. "Poppy is still so mad we couldn't go."

"I could get you guys tickets for tomorrow's show?" JoJo offered. "We always keep a few extra seats open for friends and family."

"I wish." Tad sighed. "But I'm filming late tomorrow, and by law my mom has to be on set with me, since I'm not eighteen." Tad's phone beeped and he glanced down at it. "Speaking of filming, my director wants me on set 'yesterday,'" he said with air quotes. "I better go. Good luck with your show!"

"Toodle-oo!" JoJo called after him—which made her and Miley crack up all over again.

JoJo and Miley were just heading out of the dining room to meet JoJo's mom when someone shouted her name. JoJo turned around to find Tasha jogging over to her.

"Did you see it?" she asked breathlessly.

"See what?" JoJo asked.

Tasha held up her iPad. A British tabloid was open on the screen. JoJo's jaw dropped when she read the headline. *The Ultimate Siwa-Sighting: JoJo Siwa Sightsees in Costume!*

The article showed a picture of a girl standing in front of the Tower of London. She had JoJo's blond side ponytail, and was wearing JoJo's missing costume . . . except she was not JoJo.

"Did you go to the Tower of London this morning?" Tasha asked her.

"I haven't even left the hotel today!" JoJo said. She looked closer at the photo. It captured the girl from the side. From that angle, whoever it was really was the spitting image of JoJo. And apparently she thought like JoJo too. The Tower of London was where the crown jewels were kept. It was number one on JoJo's sightseeing list.

"You weren't kidding about that costume," Miley said. "It is super special."

JoJo studied the costume in the picture. The long, sequined cape that she worked so hard on with Kyra and Goldie Chic shimmered in every color of the rainbow. Underneath the cape was a short dress made entirely out of feathers in a matching rainbow pattern. The breeze lifted some of the feathers, making the dress look like a bird about to take flight. "It's everything I hoped it would be," JoJo said. "Except I'm not the one wearing it!"

"But it kind of looks like you are," Tasha said. "I guess you have a doppelgänger, JoJo."

"And we have to find her," Miley said.

"I know our first sightseeing stop," JoJo said. "Tower of London, here we come!"

CHAPTER 6

"This place is mega cool," Miley said.

"I think you mean *jolly good*," JoJo corrected with a laugh. JoJo, Miley, and Mrs. Siwa were standing in front of the Tower of London. With its towers and spires and dozens of arched windows, all surrounded by a real, now-empty moat, it looked like something straight out of a fairy tale. Several guards were stationed out front in fancy red and gold uniforms, complete with furry black hats.

"Those guards look very serious," Miley whispered to JoJo.

"And stylish," JoJo added.

"According to my guidebook, when the Tower of London was first built in the 1070s, it was the most secure castle in the land," Miley said. "It guarded the royals and their possessions during war. But later on, it had a lot of other purposes. It was a prison for a while, and at one point it was even a royal zoo that housed exotic animals!"

"I prefer jewels," JoJo said with a giggle.

"You'll certainly see lots of them in the Jewel House," JoJo's mom assured her.

"The Jewel House has a real working collection of royal regalia," Miley recited. "According to my guidebook, that means the Queen actually uses pieces that are stored here for ceremonies."

"That's so cool!" JoJo squealed.

JoJo's mom bought tickets, and they headed over to the Jewel House. "It's like walking into one of my dreams," JoJo said. Everywhere she looked, there were glass cases containing dozens of crowns and other royal regalia—all covered in real gemstones! "Rubies and emeralds and diamonds, oh my," JoJo breathed. She stopped to read a plaque. "Did you know there are over twenty thousand jewels in this collection?"

"Sounds like your wardrobe, JoJo," Miley said with a laugh.

"Why don't you girls look around a bit?" Mrs. Siwa suggested. "I'll ask the guards if they saw our mystery girl this morning."

JoJo didn't have to be told twice. She couldn't help but gape at all the jewels. This place was sparkle city! She stopped in front of a case that held a dazzling crown encrusted with hundreds of diamonds and the largest sapphire she'd ever seen. "That would look good with one of my costumes," JoJo said.

"So would this." Miley pointed to a crown featuring a mix of sapphires, emeralds, pearls, and rubies.

"Ooh yes," JoJo agreed. "Or this one would do too." She showed Miley a crown made entirely out of glittering diamonds. "If only I could get the Queen to lend one of these to me!" she joked.

They kept walking through the Jewel House, admiring the crowns, swords, robes, and orbs—all dazzling with jewels. "Whoa, what's that?" JoJo asked. She stopped in front of a gorgeous, bejeweled stick with an enormous diamond in the center. "It looks like the fanciest walking stick I've ever seen!"

"Oh, I saw a picture of that in my guidebook!" Miley said. "It's a scepter. It's held by a monarch during a coronation."

JoJo read the plaque next to the scepter. "Wow, this scepter has the largest clear-cut diamond in the world. It's over 530 carats!"

JoJo and Miley were still admiring the scepter when JoJo heard her mom calling them. "Hey, girls! Come here!" JoJo's mom waved them over to where she was standing with an enormous guard. He had muscles that nearly bulged out of his shirt, and a stern expression on his face.

"I wouldn't want to mess with him," Miley whispered in JoJo's ear.

"Samesies," JoJo whispered back.

"Guess what," Mrs. Siwa said excitedly. "Mr. Jones here saw your doppelgänger this morning! Tell them what you told me, Mr. Jones."

The guard surprised JoJo by giving them the slightest of smiles. "The person of interest arrived in a tour group at approximately

10:07 A.M. She was wearing an extravagant outfit—I quite fancied it," he added. JoJo tried really hard not to giggle as she exchanged a look with Miley. "A gaggle of kids was following her around like ducklings," Mr. Jones continued. He paused and cocked his head, studying JoJo. "Actually, she looked a lot like a younger version of you," he said. "You might even call her a mini you."

JoJo froze. "What did you say?"

"A mini you," Mr. Jones repeated. "Just a little British humor."

JoJo's mind was suddenly spinning. A girl who looked like a younger JoJo . . . A mini her . . . An image of Cassie flashed through her mind. The dancers all called her "MiniJo."

Could it be . . . ? Was it possible . . . ?

No! Cassie was like a little sister to her! She would never have stolen her costume.

Right?

JoJo looked at Miley. From the nervous way Miley was biting her bottom lip, JoJo wondered if she was thinking the exact same thing. "Did you hear the girl say anything that might help us find her?" Miley asked. "Maybe where she was headed? My friend has a performance tomorrow"— Miley pointed at JoJo—"and that girl has her costume!"

Mr. Jones shook his head. "Not really— though, I did see her ask Mark something . . . Hey, Mark!" He called over to a smaller, older guard standing in the corner by a bejeweled sword. "That girl in the fancy outfit earlier . . . What did she ask you?"

"She wanted to know how far we were from the London Eye," Mark replied. "I think her tour group was heading there next. Why?"

JoJo didn't listen to Mr. Jones's response. She was too busy whipping around to face her mom. "The London Eye is the huge Ferris wheel, right?"

"It is," Mrs. Siwa confirmed.

"According to my guidebook, it's Europe's tallest Ferris wheel," Miley chimed in.

JoJo looked from her mom to Miley. "I guess we found our next sightseeing stop."

JoJo looked out the window as a taxi carried them through London. Incredible sights flew past outside. "Look at that!" she exclaimed. She pointed to a garden that had grown up around old stone ruins. Sunlight streamed through huge stone archways, which were covered in trails of ivy and climbing flowers. "It looks like a secret garden."

"That's the St. Dunstan-in-the-East ruins," their taxi driver informed them. "The old church ruins have become a public garden."

"There's nothing like that at home," JoJo said.

"For real," Miley agreed. "Everything is so much older here!"

They drove past restaurants and parks and monuments and picturesque European streets. When they drove over the Southwark Bridge, the River Thames glittered beneath them. Finally their taxi pulled up to a huge Ferris wheel. "We've arrived at the London Eye!" their taxi driver announced.

JoJo, Miley, and JoJo's mom gaped at the huge Ferris wheel as they climbed out of the taxi. Dozens of large, oval-shaped glass capsules hung from it. The bench inside those capsules gave the riders a bird's-eye view of the city.

"They look like little spaceships," JoJo said, admiring the capsules.

"Yeah, that thing is fierce," Miley said. "We definitely need to ride it!"

"And what better way to search for my impersonator than with a view of the whole city?" In spite of her missing costume, JoJo had to admit she was excited. Taking a ride on the London Eye wasn't exactly something you got to do every day!

"Should we get three tickets, Mom?" JoJo asked. "Hey, what's wrong, Mom?"

JoJo's mom was frozen in place, staring up in horror at the enormous Ferris wheel. "So . . . high . . . " she murmured.

"Oh, right!" JoJo said. "My mom doesn't love heights," she informed Miley. "Looks like we're on our own here."

"Let's do this," Miley said.

"Have . . . fun," Mrs. Siwa managed to say with a shudder. She gave JoJo money for the tickets. JoJo loved seeing money from different countries. British pounds looked so much fancier than American dollars! "Be careful!" her mom called after them, as she went to wait on a nearby bench. "Hold on tight!"

"Mom, we'll be *inside* a capsule!" JoJo called back with a giggle.

The line was short, and soon JoJo and Miley were climbing inside one of the big glass capsules. A group of adults sat next to them, chattering away excitedly in French. JoJo squeezed Miley's arm as their capsule rose higher and higher into the air. Unlike her mom, she liked heights. She loved feeling like she was part of the sky.

"What a great view of Big Ben!" Miley squealed. She pointed to the famous clock tower that rose above the Thames. "It looks just like the pictures in my guide-book. Ooh, and there's Buckingham Palace!"

Miley pointed at the sprawling castle in the distance.

"And look at that." JoJo pointed in the other direction at a beautiful building with a big, round dome on top. "Isn't that St. Paul's Cathedral?"

"Yup," Miley confirmed. "According to my guidebook, it's one of the largest domes in the world, and it has this really cool whispering gallery. Sound travels so well in its dome that even if we stood on opposite sides and I whispered super quietly, you'd still be able to hear me!"

"I want to try that!" JoJo said.

Miley looked like she was about to agree, but then she stopped. "First we've got to focus. More sequins, less sightseeing!"

"You're right. At least my impersonator is wearing something you can't exactly miss,"

JoJo joked. She pressed her forehead against the glass and scanned for bursts of rainbow below. "Hey, Miley," she said as she searched. "Remember what the guard said back at the Tower of London, about this impersonator being a mini me? Did that make you think of anyone?"

"Cassie?" Miley asked quietly.

"Yeah." JoJo sighed. "But she wouldn't . . . would she?"

"She has always wanted to be just like you," Miley pointed out.

"But in like a little sister way!" JoJo protested.

JoJo and Miley kept searching until everyone below was as small as ants. "I didn't see any sequins," Miley said.

"Or feathers," JoJo added.

Miley sighed. "This girl is good, whoever she is."

Suddenly JoJo's phone beeped. "Tasha texted me," she said. She held out her phone so Miley could read the text with her.

Did you see the latest comment on your missing dress post?!?

Miley looked at JoJo. "What comment?"

JoJo quickly pulled up the livestreamed video from her dressing room and scrolled down to the last comment.

XTinaXOXO: Just saw you heading into Buckingham Palace in the MOST ULTRA AMAZING costume. So glad you found it, JoJo!!! XOXO

"Buckingham Palace," Miley breathed.

"It looks like Mini Me is still a step ahead of real me," JoJo said.

"Well, I guess we'll just have to *drag* ourselves to the famous Buckingham Palace to catch her." Miley grinned. "Which, according to my guidebook, is where the Queen of England actually lives!"

"In that case, I think we're going to need some royal accessories." As the Ferris wheel lowered them back to the ground, JoJo pointed to a booth selling glittery plastic tiaras. She smiled at her best friend. "We're going to catch this thief in style!"

CHAPTER 7

"After you, your highness," JoJo's mom said with a dramatic curtsy.

JoJo touched the fake diamond-and-sapphire tiara perched on her head. "Don't think a curtsy can get you out of wearing one, Mom." She stood on her toes to place a fake ruby tiara on her mom's head. "Royally perfect," she declared.

"Jolly good, really," Miley added with a grin. She had gone full emerald with her tiara, and the fake green stones sparkled against her dark hair.

They all climbed into the backseat of a taxi. "Please deliver these princesses to Buckingham Palace!" Mrs. Siwa asked the driver in her best English accent. "We're going to visit the Queen!"

"Tourists," the driver muttered under his breath, which made JoJo and Miley dissolve into a fit of giggles. "Just so you know, no one's allowed to actually go inside Buckingham Palace today," their driver added, more loudly this time. "Do you still want to go?"

"Oh, that's right!" Miley said. "Buckingham Palace is only open to guests during the summer months, when the Queen isn't living there."

"According to your guidebook?" JoJo teased.

Miley nodded. "You know it."

"So how did your impostor get inside?" Mrs. Siwa wondered aloud. JoJo had filled her in on the latest update while they purchased their tiaras.

"Only one way to find out," JoJo replied. "We still want to go," she informed the driver.

As London passed by in a blur outside her window, something kept nagging at JoJo. Something about Buckingham Palace . . . "Of course!" she said. Or maybe she shouted it, because everyone in the taxi jumped. "Sorry. I just remembered something. Didn't Tad say he was filming at Buckingham Palace today?"

"Good memory!" Miley exclaimed. "I was so distracted by all the sights, I totally forgot about that."

"So what does that mean?" Mrs. Siwa asked. She adjusted her tiara, looking as confused as JoJo felt.

"I have no idea," JoJo admitted.

Soon, the driver was pulling up to Buckingham Palace. "That's the visitors' entrance," he said, pointing to tall iron gates emblazoned with two huge gold crests. "But like I said, it's closed."

JoJo couldn't help but gape as they climbed out of the taxi. The beautiful white stone palace loomed behind the iron gates. It was enormous and stately, with tall columns and row after row of windows. "There must be hundreds of rooms in there!" JoJo said.

"Seven hundred and seventy-five to be exact," Miley said. "According—"

"To your guidebook," JoJo and Mrs. Siwa finished together.

Miley giggled. "Look at those." She pointed to two large white trailers.

"Those are movie trailers," Mrs. Siwa said. "They must be for the film."

JoJo walked over to a sign posted nearby. "This says you need a *Nine Lives* identification badge to enter the palace. So that means my impersonator must be involved with the *Nine Lives* movie somehow."

"At least that rules out Cassie," Miley offered.

"Why don't we go see what we can find out," Mrs. Siwa said. She led them over to the security guard posted at the entrance.

"Hi," JoJo said, flashing the guard her friendliest smile. "We're here because—"

"Badge?" the security guard interrupted.

"Well, we don't exactly have one, but—"

"No badge, no entrance," the guard barked.

"But—" JoJo tried again.

"No buts," the guard added.

JoJo looked at Miley. "What now?" she mouthed.

Before Miley could answer, JoJo's mom

nudged her. "Isn't that the actor you were talking to in The Worchester?"

JoJo followed her mom's gaze. Tad Harwell was walking out of Buckingham Palace, wearing a fancy white suit with gold epaulets on his shoulders. "Hey, Tad! Tad!" In the distance, she saw Tad spin around, looking confused. "Over here, Tad!" JoJo waved her arms. "By the gate!"

When his spotted them, he broke into a smile and jogged over to greet them. "JoJo! Miley! What are you guys doing here? Actually, hold on—let me get you inside." He turned to the security guard. "They're my on-set guests," he said. "You can let them through." Without another word, the security guard unlocked the gate and stepped aside.

"Thank you so much," JoJo said as Tad waved them through the gates.

"Anything for my sister's favorite singer. Nice tiaras," Tad added with a grin. "But what exactly are you guys doing here? Wait—are you following me?" he teased. "Because that would be my sister's dream. She is going to be so mad that she missed you *again*."

"I'm starting to wonder if you even really have a sister," JoJo joked. "But in all seriousness, we're here because of my missing costume." She quickly filled him in on how the search for her costume led them here. "I know this sounds crazy, but can you think of anyone on the film who might have stolen my costume?"

Tad shook his head. "I really can't. Besides, I'm the youngest one on set. Even Haley Crest, who plays the main character, Laurette, is actually twenty in real life. And she has black hair, not blond."

JoJo sighed. "I don't get it. Do you think we can take a look around and see what we find?"

"Sure. I have a scene coming up, but I can get badges for you guys so you can look around the set."

"Wow," Miley said admiringly. "You've got clout."

"Well, I *am* George." Tad led them toward the entrance of the palace. It was even more incredible up close. The building was enormous! It was built in a rectangle, with an open courtyard in the middle. An immaculate green yard spread out behind it, surrounded by trees.

"I thought your name was Tad?" Mrs. Siwa asked, looking confused.

"George is my character in the film," Tad explained.

"Oh em gee, Mrs. Siwa. Do you not know the story of *Nine Lives*?" Miley burst out.

Mrs. Siwa laughed. "I can't say I do."

"Well, thanks to Grace, I can quote it even better than my guidebook," Miley said. "There's this girl, Laurette, who lives in an orphanage in London. And on her sixteenth birthday she receives a mysterious amulet."

"It turns out the amulet has the power to show her nine different versions of her life," JoJo jumped in.

"In one version, she's part of an enormous farming family in the countryside," Miley continued. "In another, she's living at a fancy Swiss boarding school."

"In my favorite version, she's a famous singer," JoJo said.

"I like the one where she's the Princess of England," Miley said.

"That's the scene we're filming at Buckingham Palace today," Tad explained.

"Ahh, so cool!" Miley squealed.

"In every version of Laurette's life, only one thing remains the same," JoJo said. "She keeps meeting this boy named George."

"Played by me." Tad gestured at his costume. "Which explains the princely suit."

"Got it," Mrs. Siwa said, looking slightly less confused. "Or, at least some of it."

At the front of Buckingham Palace, Tad waved to another set of security guards, who stepped aside to let them in. JoJo held her breath as she walked into the palace. It all came out in one long rush as she looked around. Intricate golden railings curved along a red-carpeted stairwell. The ceiling soared high above them, and gilded paintings and gold carvings adorned the walls. It was by far the fanciest place she'd ever been. And to top it off, at the bottom of the elaborate staircase was a bustling movie set.

Miley clutched JoJo's arm. "Is that Nicola Anister?" she gasped. JoJo pointed to a beautiful blond woman who was talking to a man with a clipboard. Several cameramen jostled around them.

"She plays my aunt in this scene," Tad explained.

JoJo gaped at Miley. Even her mom looked at little starstruck. Nicola Anister was one of the most famous actresses in the world. "So I guess this is a pretty big movie, huh?" her mom said.

"Um, yeah." Miley laughed. "Like the biggest."

"Even my mom got all tongue-twisted when she met Nicola," Tad said. He pointed to a woman sitting in a director's chair across the set. She had the same wavy brown hair and bright blue eyes as Tad. "And she's met almost as many actors as I have."

"Tad! We need you on set!" the man with the clipboard yelled.

"The director calls," Tad told them. "But here." He went over to a bag and pulled out three badges that said NINE LIVES VISITORS PASS. "Feel free to look around."

JoJo watched Tad hurry off to set. When the director called "action," it was like Tad instantly transformed. Outgoing, cheerful Tad Harwell was gone, and mischievous George Evans, with his trademark smirk, was in his place.

"I see why he gets the big roles," Mrs. Siwa whispered.

They headed away from set, where their voices wouldn't distract the actors. "Why don't we divide and conquer again, girls?"

Mrs. Siwa suggested. "I'll go this way, you two go that way?" She gestured to opposite sides of the palace. "Meet back here in twenty?"

JoJo nodded. "Text if you see anything!"

"I know we need to look for your costume, JoJo," Miley said, as Mrs. Siwa disappeared around the corner. "But what do you think about FaceTiming Grace first?"

"I was thinking the exact same thing," JoJo said. "She is going to *freak out* when she sees this!" JoJo pulled out her phone and quickly calculated the time at home. "It's just late enough to call her."

Grace was sitting at her kitchen table eating a bowl of cereal when she answered. "Hi! I miss you guys! I was actually just wondering what exciting things you were up to while I'm sitting here eating my boring bowl of cereal." She broke into a smile, and JoJo felt a sudden pang of homesickness. She missed her friends! And her dad and her brother. But she reminded herself that one of the best parts of traveling was how great it was to see everyone when she got home.

"We miss you too, Grace," she said. "We have a little surprise for you, but you have to be really quiet when we show you. Actually, that's probably going to be impossible so . . ." She lowered the volume on her phone to zero. "Now you can be as loud as you want." Quietly, JoJo crept back toward the *Nine Lives* set. When she was close enough to get a good view, she flipped her phone around for Grace to see.

JoJo watched as Grace absorbed the scene in front of her. Tad Harwell and Nicola Anister were walking toward them, filming. Instantly, recognition dawned on Grace's face. Her jaw dropped and, even though the sound was off on JoJo's phone, she was a thousand percent sure that Grace was shrieking at the top of her lungs. She let her friend watch for another minute before quietly backing away from the set.

Miley led the way up the grand staircase and toward the first open door they saw. JoJo flashed their new badges, and a security guard let them in. The room was huge, with dozens of chandeliers hanging from the ceiling and an elaborate carved arch on one side. Normally, it looked like it would be some kind of ballroom, but right now temporary walls transformed it into several dressing rooms.

The instant JoJo turned her phone volume back on, she heard Grace's shrieks. "What is going on?" Grace exclaimed. "Are you on the *Nine Lives* set? How? Why? Tell me everything!"

"It's a long story, and we don't have a lot of time," Miley said. "But yes, we're on the set, and we met Tad Harwell!"

JoJo quickly lowered her volume again as Grace's shrieks pierced the room. She waited until Grace looked more composed to turn it back up. "I cannot believe this," Grace said. "You do a lot of cool things, JoJo, but this might be the coolest one ever! I'm so jealous. You have to take a picture with Tad for me! And Nicola! And the set! And—"

Nearby, a woman rolled a rack of costumes past, and gave them an annoyed look.

"Maybe we should move," Miley suggested.

They went deeper into the enormous room, to a back corner where a stack of costume supplies was stored. There were bolts of fabric and spools of thread and a whole bin of royal accessories. "We're actually here on an investigation," JoJo told Grace. "We think my costume thief is on set somewhere."

"Who do you think it could be?" Grace asked breathlessly.

"That's the thing," JoJo said. "We have no idea! The only actors we saw were Tad and Nicola, and according to Tad, the rest of the cast and crew are adults . . ." Suddenly she trailed off. "Hey, guys, what is that?" She went over to a bin of fake tiaras.

"They look kind of like our tiaras," Miley said.

"I meant to tell you that I like the royal look you have going on," Grace teased.

"Not the tiaras," JoJo said. "The feather!"

She knelt down and plucked a purple feather out from between two tiaras. It was covered in a dusting of gold glitter—just like the feathers from her costume. "Goldie Chic had to use a complicated hand-application process to get the feathers dusted in glitter like this. There's no way they have the *exact same* ones on the movie set! This must have come from the thief!"

"Hey, look over there." Miley pointed toward the row of dressing rooms. Lying on the floor was a glittery blue feather. "It's another one!"

"And is that a sequin?" JoJo gasped. She and Miley followed the trail of sequins and feathers until they were standing directly in front of one of the dressing rooms. There was a name posted on the dressing room door. TAD HARWELL.

JoJo exchanged a confused look with Miley. "Go in," Grace urged.

JoJo felt a little guilty as she turned the knob to Tad's dressing room door. "We'll just peek inside really quickly," she promised herself. "I'm sure we won't find anything . . ."

But once more, she trailed off as she stepped into the dressing room. There, draped over a chair, was JoJo's full costume. Both the dress and cape had small tears down the side. "I can't believe it," JoJo gasped.

"What?" Grace asked from the phone screen. "What is it?"

JoJo flipped the phone around so Grace could see. "It looks like Tad Harwell stole my costume."

CHAPTER 8

"Tad Harwell stole your costume?" Grace screeched from the phone. "Why? That makes no sense."

"It really doesn't," JoJo agreed. "Especially since he acted like he had no idea what I was talking about earlier!"

"Well, he is a great actor," Miley pointed out. "We saw that firsthand."

"Still . . ." JoJo shook her head. "It doesn't add up. Why would he bring us on set and let us wander around if he knew we could stumble upon the costume in his dressing room? And why would—?"

JoJo didn't get to finish that thought, because suddenly, she heard footsteps. They were walking in the direction of Tad's dressing room. She exchanged a frantic look with Miley.

"We're probably not supposed to be in the star of the movie's dressing room," Miley said nervously.

The footsteps drew closer. JoJo could hear the people talking. "I have something to show you," said a girl. Her voice was tense. "It's not good."

"What is it?" a woman replied. "Are you still feeling sick? Do you need to lie down?"

"That's the thing . . . I wasn't actually sick," the girl said. The footsteps stopped in front of Tad's dressing room. JoJo looked frantically around, but in the makeshift dressing room, there was nowhere to hide. The door flew open. A small girl wearing a huge sparkly bow on top of her blond ponytail walked in. "I was actually—" she was saying, but when she saw JoJo and Miley, she fell abruptly silent. She looked like she was about to faint. "JoJo . . . JOJO SIWA?" she shrieked. "What—how— OH EM GEE!"

A woman with wavy dark hair and piercing blue eyes stood next to her. JoJo recognized her. It was Tad's mom! The girl must be his little sister, Poppy!

"What's going on here?" Mrs. Harwell asked, looking very confused.

"Hi." JoJo stepped forward. "I'm JoJo Siwa and this is my friend, Miley." Miley gave a sheepish wave. "Oh, and Grace!" She held up her phone, and Grace waved from the screen. "We're here because—"

97

"Your costume," Poppy whispered. JoJo nodded. Tears filled Poppy's eyes as she turned to her mom. "This was what I was trying to tell you. I—I did a terrible thing." With that, she burst into tears.

One after another, puzzle pieces clicked together in JoJo's brain. Poppy looked a lot like a young JoJo . . . Tad had told JoJo his sister was a superfan . . . JoJo's costume was found in Poppy's brother's dressing room . . . JoJo gasped.

"I'm so, so sorry," Poppy choked out.

At that moment, Tad walked into the room, followed by Mrs. Siwa. At the sight of Tad, Grace let out a sudden squeal on the phone, then tried to cover it up with a cough. Tad furrowed his brow. "Poppy? JoJo?" His eyes landed on the sparkly costume draped over his chair. "Is that your missing costume, JoJo? What's going on?"

"I have the same question," Mrs. Siwa said.

Mrs. Harwell put her arm around her daughter. "I think Poppy has something to tell us," she said gently.

Poppy took a deep breath and wiped her eyes. "It all started when I found out JoJo Siwa was going to be performing while we were in London," she said shakily. "I was beyond super excited, but when I told my mom, she said that Tad was filming long hours that week, which meant he had to be on set late, which meant *she* had to be on set late, which meant there was no one to take me to the show. It was just so frustrating! I'm a singer too, and JoJo is my hero! Seeing her in concert has always been my dream!" She flashed JoJo a quivering smile. "But did anyone care? Of course not. Because everything's always about Tad and his movies."

She looked at her brother. "Sorry, Tad. I'm so proud of you and everything you've accomplished. You know I am! But sometimes it feels like I'm invisible when you're around. I was just so upset that you and mom didn't realize how important this concert was to me! And then you saw JoJo at the hotel, and I didn't! It all felt so unfair."

Poppy's mom shook her head as she listened to her daughter. "But Poppy—" she began.

Poppy held up a hand to stop her. "Let me get this all out," she whispered. She took a deep breath. "When I found out JoJo's concert was at one of the locations where Tad was filming this week, I knew I had to do something. The night of the concert, you were both so distracted by Tad's scene that I realized no one would even notice if I was gone. So I took a *Nine Lives* pass and snuck out. All I had to do was flash my movie pass and the guard at the Royal Albert Hall let me in."

"I just wanted to see JoJo for myself!" Poppy continued. "But when I got there, I couldn't find her backstage. So I kind of, maybe . . . thought I would take a tiny peek at her dressing room. I wasn't planning to stay long, I swear! But then I saw her garment bag and I just *had* to take a look at her super-secret costume. I couldn't believe how gorgeous it was. I thought maybe it wouldn't hurt to try it on, just for one quick second."

"Poppy!" Tad admonished. "I can't believe you did that."

Poppy hung her head. "I know it was wrong. But I promise I was just planning to try it on, take a picture, and put it back," she said quietly. "But then I heard footsteps coming, and I knew I had to get it off right away. I was hurrying so much that I got the dress's zipper caught on one of the feathers! I tried to fix it, but it was really stuck. I couldn't take it off without destroying the whole costume. Someone was coming closer, so I panicked! I shoved my own sweatshirt into the garment bag and raced out of Royal Albert Hall as fast as I could. I didn't mean to steal your costume, JoJo! I swear! It just sort of . . . happened." Tears welled up in Poppy's eyes again.

JoJo rubbed her forehead as she digested everything Poppy had told them. "There's something I still don't understand, though. Why were you still wearing my costume the next day? And all over London?"

"Well, I raced right back to my hotel room after I left your dressing room. I figured if I could take my time, I could get the costume off. But I was wrong. The dress ripped," Poppy said miserably. "I couldn't believe what I had done! So the next morning, I told my mom I wasn't feeling well and wanted to stay in the hotel to rest."

"That was a lie?" Mrs. Harwell jumped in.

"Yes," Poppy murmured. "Instead, I asked the hotel to send a tailor up. It's actually pretty amazing the things a hotel like The Worchester will help you with," she added, brightening for a second. "The tailor was great and she fixed the dress! She asked me to put it back on to double-check it, and it was perfect!" Poppy looked down. "It really is your best costume ever, JoJo. Wearing it made me feel so special, I—I just wanted someone to see me in it! My plan was to go down to the lobby for five minutes, maybe show a porter or two. But then I ran into those twin girls, Lizzy and Sophie. Remember them? The ones we sat with at The Worchester's Tea and Tiaras event? When they saw me, they went nuts! They thought I was so cool in that costume. It was just so fun. I didn't feel invisible at all anymore."

"When The Worchester's tour bus pulled up, Lizzy and Sophie begged me to go on the daily tour so their friends could see my costume too. And I just—I couldn't help myself! For one day, I wanted to be the one who got all the attention. I wanted to feel important!" She hung her head. "I know how wrong it was. I'm really sorry."

"Poppy, you're always important, no matter what you're wearing," Tad said, hugging his sister. "I'm sorry you were feeling so ignored."

"Tad's right, honey." Mrs. Harwell stroked her daughter's hair. "What you did was really wrong, and dangerous! And we're going to have a long talk about the consequences later. But I never want you to feel like you don't matter."

Poppy nodded. Tears streamed down her face as she turned to JoJo. "I'm sorry I messed up your costume, JoJo. You're my idol! I never meant to hurt you . . ." She trailed off. She was crying too hard to talk.

JoJo waited to feel angry, but as she watched Poppy cry and clutch her big brother, she just felt sad. She knew sometimes it could be hard for her own friends and family that she got so much attention. "I agree that you made a mistake, Poppy. But I bet it can be hard to be the sister of a famous actor. Even though I don't mean to, I sometimes take attention away from my friends or family, just by being there. It's one of my least favorite parts of getting recognized so often."

"I guess that happens around me too," Tad said. "I never really thought about it before."

"Sometimes when you're around, Tad, it's like people stop seeing me as *me*," Poppy explained. "I'm just your little sister."

"I get it," Miley said gently. "Believe me—I'm JoJo Siwa's best friend! What helps is spending time doing something you're great at, something that's just for you. Like singing," she suggested. "Didn't you say you like to sing?"

Poppy brightened instantly. "It's my favorite thing in the world."

"Hey, I have an idea," JoJo said suddenly. "Sing something for me!"

Poppy looked around nervously. "Right here? Right now? In front of the one and only JoJo Siwa?"

JoJo laughed. "Yup." Miley fiddled with her phone and soon the first few notes of "Boomerang" rang out.

"Okay . . ." Poppy's voice was shaky, but as she launched into the song, her nerves fell away. Her voice was clear and beautiful as it rang through the room.

"Girl, you can sing!" JoJo exclaimed when Poppy finished the song.

Poppy beamed. "That means everything coming from you, JoJo."

"I have a plan I think you're going to like," JoJo said.

"Uh-oh," Miley said a laugh.

"Double uh-oh," Mrs. Siwa agreed.

"Don't worry." JoJo grinned. "I think you're all going to like this." She turned to Mrs. Harwell. "If you're okay with my mom taking Poppy to my concert"—she paused and looked questioningly at her mom, who nodded her approval—"then I'd love Poppy to come up onstage to sing a song with me. Would you like that, Poppy?"

"Oh em gee!" Poppy leapt across the room and flung herself at JoJo in a huge hug. "I wouldn't like that. I'd *love* it!" Poppy turned to her mom. "Is it okay, Mom? Please please pretty please with a thousand sparkly bows on top?"

"You really are a true Siwanator," JoJo said with a laugh. "What do you say, Mrs. Harwell? Can Poppy help me out at my concert?"

"Well . . ." Mrs. Harwell hesitated. "You're still in big trouble, Poppy. What you did was wrong, and not safe! You're much too young to be taking a tour of London by yourself! Even if it was on our hotel's tour bus. We're going to have a long conversation later, and will have to discuss an appropriate consequence."

"I know," Poppy murmured.

"But in the meantime . . . if JoJo's mom doesn't mind watching you, then I'm okay with you going to the concert."

"Thank you thank you thank you!" Poppy jumped up and down so hard that her sparkly bow fell off.

"Looks like you Siwanator'ed too hard," Grace called out from the phone. Everyone laughed.

"Oh, that reminds me. Tad, this is my friend, Grace, the *Nine Lives* superfan." JoJo held up the phone so Tad could see Grace.

"Nice to meet you, Grace." Tad's trademark dimple flashed as he smiled hello.

"I—you—nice—Tad Harwell!" Grace blubbered.

"I think that means hello," JoJo translated. She turned back to Poppy. "I just have one last question," JoJo said. "If the tailor fixed my dress, then why do both my dress and cape have tears in them now?"

Poppy's face turned bright red. "I kind of, um, got them both stuck in the door of the tour bus."

Tad gaped at his sister. "You managed to rip JoJo's costume *twice*?"

"Yeah ... kind of," Poppy said sheepishly. "I came here because I knew there was a costume designer on set and I was hoping she could fix it. That's why I was bringing you to Tad's dressing room, Mom. To show you."

"Oh, Poppy." Mrs. Harwell shook her head, looking disappointed in her daughter. "Luckily, Poppy is right and we do have a costume designer on set. We can ask her to do us a favor and fix JoJo's costume. We'll make sure your dress is like new for your concert tomorrow, JoJo."

"I really am so sorry, JoJo," Poppy said.

"It's okay, Poppy," JoJo said gently. "The most important thing is that you finally told the truth. And it sounds like it's all going to be fixed by my concert tomorrow. So what we need to focus on now is finding you a costume of your own . . ." She winked at Poppy, who blushed as pink as her shirt.

"I don't know how I can ever thank you for being so nice to my sister," Tad said to JoJo. "Actually . . ." He paused. "Maybe I do know how. JoJo and Miley, how would you like to be extras in the next scene of *Nine Lives*?"

JoJo and Miley shared an excited look. "We wouldn't like that," JoJo said, borrowing Poppy's phrase.

"We'd *love* it!" JoJo and Miley yelled in unison.

"On set—extras—*Nine Lives*—" Grace stammered on the phone. "You have to set me up so I can watch! I don't want to miss a single thing!"

Tad laughed. "I'm sure we can arrange that. Now let's go film a movie!"

An hour later, JoJo and Miley were on the set of *Nine Lives*, dressed in extravagant ball gowns. Grace was watching from JoJo's phone, which was propped up on a director's chair nearby. "This is the big ballroom scene," the director explained to the extras. "Laurette's father has just been crowned king, and the royal family is hosting a ball to celebrate. Your job is stroll through the ballroom, talking quietly to one another as if you're guests at the ball. Got it?"

All the extras said, "Got it," but Miley and JoJo said it loudest of all.

"I wish BowBow could be here with us," JoJo said to Miley as the director stopped to talk to one of the cameramen.

"That dog does love the camera," Miley agreed.

"And the camera loves her," JoJo replied with a giggle.

Nearby, the director held up a clapboard, and JoJo, Miley, and the rest of the extras fell silent.

The director announced, "Ballroom scene, take one! Cue lighting! Cue sound! And *action!*"

"Can you believe this?" JoJo whispered to Miley as they strolled through the ballroom with their arms linked together. Up ahead, cameras swarmed Tad as he danced with Haley Crest, the actress who played Laurette, a beautiful, dark-haired girl who was new to Hollywood.

"You know what? I can," Miley whispered back. "Amazing things happen when I'm with you, JoJo!"

"This is one trip I'm never going to forget," JoJo said. "And the best part is we got to do it together."

"BFFs," Miley said.

"Best Friends Forever," JoJo agreed. "And ever."

CHAPTER 9

As the curtain rose on JoJo's final performance in London, a thrill raced through her. She was wearing her show-stopping costume—in perfect condition once again—and sitting in the front row were her mom, her best friend, her favorite dog, and her new friend, Poppy. "Hello, London!" she cheered, looking out over the packed house. "I am super excited to be here with you guys and to finally be wearing my surprise costume!"

She did a twirl onstage to show off her costume. Her dress's feathers fluttered, and her cape swooped out around her, its sequins glittering and shimmering. She had no doubt the bright rainbow colors practically jumped off the stage. At the sight of the costume, the audience went wild. She caught a glimpse of BowBow barking along with them.

"It's pretty great, right? Thank you to Goldie Chic and my friend, Kyra, for helping me design it! And thank you to the costume designers on the set of the *Nine Lives* movie for helping make sure it was perfect for tonight. Now, I want to call a friend up to help me sing the first song of the night. Poppy Harwell, will you join me onstage?"

Poppy looked a little nervous as she climbed onto the stage. She was dressed in one of the dancers' costumes—with some alterations suggested by Kyra to set her apart. In her puffy tulle skirt and shiny pink leotard covered in sparkly bows, she looked like a real star.

The first few notes of "Boomerang" filled the stadium. JoJo belted out the first line of the song. Next to her, Poppy's voice was a little shakier. Suddenly JoJo spotted something amazing offstage. It was Tad and Mrs. Harwell! They'd come to watch Poppy! She gestured at Poppy to look over. At the sight of her family, Poppy lit up. Her shoulders loosened, and instantly her voice steadied.

"Something's gotta happen, and I think it's really big," they sang together. Their voices filled the stadium in perfect harmony.

When the song came to an end, the audience leapt to their feet in a standing ovation.

"Not bad for her first performance, right?" JoJo asked, which only made the audience cheer louder.

Poppy threw her arms around JoJo in a tight hug. "Thank you," she whispered. "This was the best night of my life!"

Hmmm, JoJo thought, as Poppy left the stage. *The best night of my life* . . . That sounded like it would make a good song. But she didn't have time to think about it now, because the first few notes of "Kid in a Candy Store" rang through the air. JoJo smiled at her audience, and began to sing.

MORE BOOKS AVAILABLE . . .

... BY JOJO SIWA!

![nickelodeon]

JoJo Siwa™

Singing JoJo

PLAYS JOJO'S HIT SONG "IT'S TIME TO CELEBRATE!"

THE MUST HAVE DOLL FOR ANY JOJO FAN!

Each singing doll includes a JoJo outfit, mircophone, brush and a wear and share Bow!

COLLECT THEM ALL!